The Dinosaur Next Door

First published in 2008 by
Franklin Watts
338 Euston Road
London
NW1 3BH

Franklin Watts Australia
Level 17/207 Kent Street
Sydney
NSW 2000

A CIP catalogue record for this book is available
from the British Library.

ISBN 978 0 7496 7968 2 (hbk)
ISBN 978 0 7496 7974 3 (pbk)

Series Editor: Jackie Hamley
Editor: Melanie Palmer
Series Advisor: Dr Hilary Minns
Series Designer: Peter Scoulding

Printed in China

Franklin Watts is a division of
Hachette Children's Books,
an Hachette Livre UK company.

The Dinosaur Next Door

by Joan Stimson

Illustrated by Andy Elkerton

FRANKLIN WATTS
LONDON•SYDNEY

Joan Stimson

"I think dinosaurs are fantastic fun because they come in so many different shapes and sizes."

Andy Elkerton

"I wouldn't like to find a dinosaur in my garden. Think of the mess and all the footprints everywhere. Drawing them is much safer!"

Last night from
my window, this
is what I saw ...

a red and purple
dinosaur –
a dinosaur next door!

The dinosaur ran
round and round.

9

It gave a great
big roar.

And then it looked
right up at me and
scared me even more.

I tried to back away.

But then it shouted,
"Hello Tom! It's party
time. Hooray!"

The dinosaur was
Mr May, the man
who lives next door.

"Enjoy the party,"
I called out. "You're a
smashing dinosaur!"

Notes for adults

TADPOLES are structured to provide support for newly independent readers. The stories may also be used by adults for sharing with young children.

Starting to read alone can be daunting. **TADPOLES** help by providing visual support and repeating words and phrases. These books will both develop confidence and encourage reading and rereading for pleasure.

If you are reading this book with a child, here are a few suggestions:

1. Make reading fun! Choose a time to read when you and the child are relaxed and have time to share the story.

2. Talk about the story before you start reading. Look at the cover and the blurb. What might the story be about? Why might the child like it?

3. Encourage the child to reread the story, and to retell the story in their own words, using the illustrations to remind them what has happened.

4. Discuss the story and see if the child can relate it to their own experience, or perhaps compare it to another story they know.

5. Give praise! Remember that small mistakes need not always be corrected.

If you enjoyed this book, why not try another TADPOLES story?

Sammy's Secret 978 0 7496 6890 7	**My Sister is a Witch!** 978 0 7496 6898 3	**At the End of the Garden** 978 0 7496 7303 1
Stroppy Poppy 978 0 7496 6893 8	**Little Troll** 978 0 7496 7293 5	**Bertie and the Big Balloon** 978 0 7496 7305 5
I'm Taller Than You! 978 0 7496 6894 5	**The Sad Princess** 978 0 7496 7294 2	**Pirate Pete** 978 0 7496 7304 8
Leo's New Pet 978 0 7496 6891 4	**Runny Honey** 978 0 7496 7295 9	**Hippo Isn't Happy** 978 0 7496 7884 5 *
Mop Top 978 0 7946 6895 2	**Dog Knows Best** 978 0 7496 7297 3	**Rooster's Alarm** 978 0 7496 7885 2 *
Charlie and the Castle 978 0 7496 6896 9	**Sam's Sunflower** 978 0 7496 7298 0	**Dad's Cake** 978 0 7496 7886 9 *
Over the Moon! 978 0 7496 6897 6	**My Big New Bed** 978 0 7496 7299 7	**Dinner for Fox** 978 0 7496 7887 6 *
Five Teddy Bears 978 0 7496 7292 8	**My Auntie Susan** 978 0 7496 7300 0	**Night, Night!** 978 0 7496 7888 3 *
	Bad Luck, Lucy! 978 0 7496 7302 4	**Amazing Shane** 978 0 7496 7889 0 *

* hardback